To my parents, with so much love.
Thank you for songs and happy memories
A

To my love Paul, thank you x
L. T.

First American Edition 2011
Kane Miller, A Division of EDC Publishing

Text © 2011 Atinuke
Illustrations © 2011 Lauren Tobia

Published by arrangement with Walker Books Ltd
87 Vauxhall Walk, London SE11 5HJ

Kane Miller, A Division of EDC Publishing
P.O. Box 470663
Tulsa, OK 74147-0663
www.kanemiller.com
www.edcpub.com

Library of Congress Control Number: 2010941500

Printed in Guangdong, China
1 2 3 4 5 6 7 8 9 10

ISBN: 978-1-61067-040-1

Kane Miller
A DIVISION OF EDC PUBLISHING

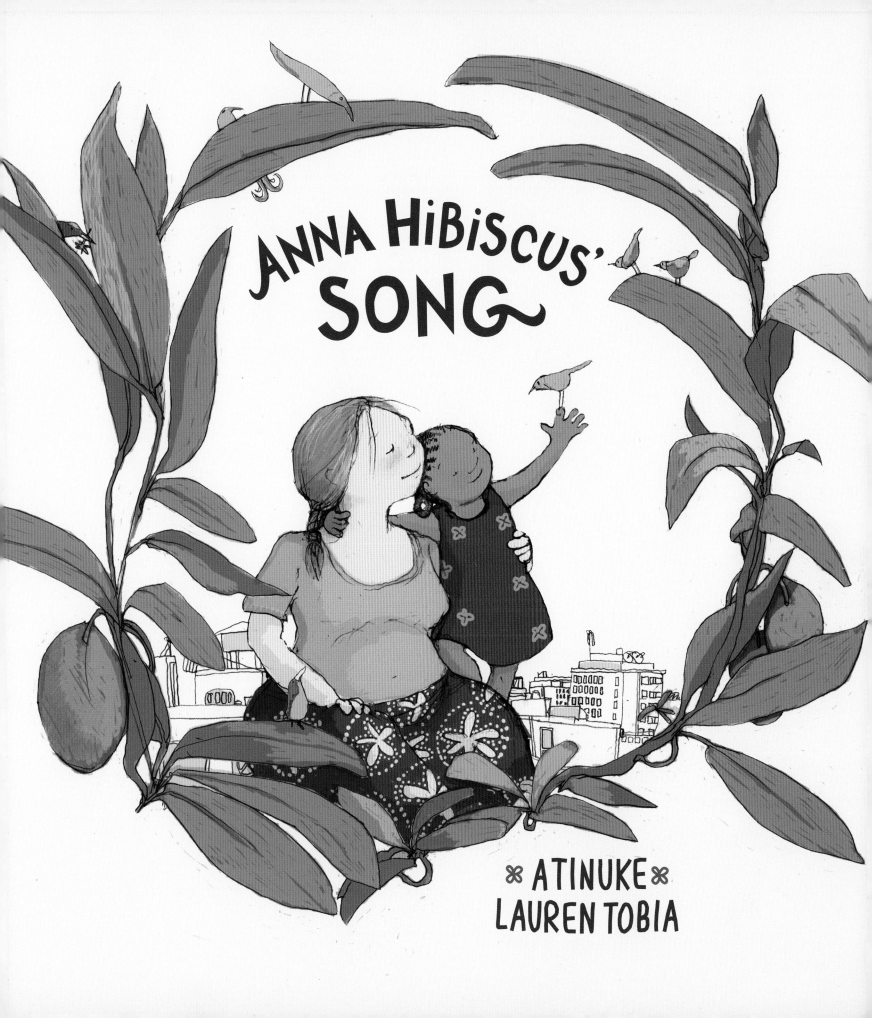

ANNA HIBISCUS' SONG

✳ ATINUKE ✳
LAUREN TOBIA

Anna Hibiscus lives in Africa.
Amazing Africa.

It is morning.
The sun is hot.
Anna Hibiscus is in the mango tree.
The tree is cool.

Up in the tree, Anna Hibiscus can see her whole family.

Grandmother and Grandfather are sitting on the veranda.

Aunties are pounding yam outside the kitchen.

Cousins are scattering corn for the chickens.

Papa is going to work with Uncle Tunde, and Mama is waving goodbye.

Anna Hibiscus feels so happy, she almost floats out of the tree.

Quickly, Anna Hibiscus jumps down.

"Grandmother!
Grandfather!"
Anna Hibiscus shouts.
"I'm so happy!
What can I do?"

Grandfather opens his hand wide.
"When I am happy, I count all the reasons why," he says.

Anna Hibiscus counts one, two, three, four, five fingers.
But she is far more happy than that!

"When I am happy," chuckles Grandmother,
"I squeeze Grandfather's hand."

So Anna Hibiscus does ...
and her happiness grows!

"Auntie Joli!" calls Anna Hibiscus.
        "I am so happy!
                What can I do?"

"You can come and help your aunties to pound yam!"
  shouts Auntie Joli.

  Anna Hibiscus is not sure.
"O-ya, come on!" the aunties laugh. "Our happiness
  gives us the strength to work. Let us see you try!"

So Anna Hibiscus tries ...

and tries ...

and tries to pound yam.

Her aunties laugh and laugh
and laugh …

and Anna Hibiscus' happiness grows!

"Anna, come and play!" call the cousins.

So Anna Hibiscus runs to Chocolate
and Angel and Benz.

"I'm so happy!" she shouts.

"What can I do?"

Chocolate says, "When I am happy, I walk on my hands!"

"I cartwheel!" says Angel.

"I somersault!" says Benz.

So Anna Hibiscus tries
to walk on her hands ...

and cartwheel ...

and somersault …

and oh! Anna Hibiscus' happiness grows!

"Anna Hibiscus! What is going on?"
        laughs Uncle Tunde.

"Oh, Uncle Tunde!"
        says Anna Hibiscus.
"I am so happy, I don't know what to do."

"O-ya!" says Uncle Tunde, turning on the car radio.
"When I am happy, I dance!"

Uncle Tunde and Anna Hibiscus
dance and dance
around the car.

And oh!
oh!
oh!
Anna Hibiscus' happiness grows!

"Papa! Papa!
What can I do?"
laughs Anna Hibiscus.
"I am SO happy, soon I will pop like a balloon."

"When I am happy," Papa smiles, "I go to Mama
and tell her how much I love her."

So Anna Hibiscus runs to her mother and says
(because it is true),
"Mama, I love you so much!"

And her mother says, "I love you so much too,
Anna Hibiscus."

And oh! Anna's happiness grows SO big!

"Mama! Mama!"
cries Anna Hibiscus.
"I am so happy,
I think I am going to
EXPLODE!"

"Then sit quietly,"
smiles Anna's mother.
"I sit still and quiet
when I am happy."

Anna Hibiscus climbs back up into the mango tree.

She sits still.

She sits quiet.

Anna Hibiscus sits
SO still and SO quiet
that the birds in the sky
fly into the branches
of the tree
and start to sing.

*That is what I can do
when I am happy!*
thinks Anna Hibiscus.

She opens her mouth wide.
And sings…

"Grandfather counts
fingers and toes.

Grandmother holds
Grandfather's hand.

Aunties work, cousins play,
Uncle dances – all day long.

Papa whispers into Mama's ear.
Mama sits so quiet and still.

And me – I sing, I sing!
I sing my happiness song!"

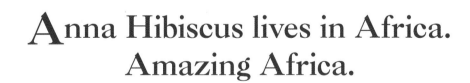

Anna Hibiscus lives in Africa.
Amazing Africa.

Anna Hibiscus is amazing too.